MW01627244

WOLVES
5
WOLVES
30

MINNESOTA TIMBERWOLVES

RICHARD RAMBECK

COVER AND TITLE PAGE PHOTOS BY MATT MAHURIN

CREATIVE EDUCATION

Published by Creative Education, Inc.
123 S. Broad Street, Mankato, Minnesota 56001 USA

Art Director, Rita Marshall
Cover and title page photography by Matt Mahurin
Book design by Rita Marshall

Photos by: Allsport; Mel Bailey; Bettmann Archive; Brian Drake; Duomo; Focus On Sports; FPG; South Florida Images Inc.; Spectra-Action; Sportschrome; Sports Photo Masters, Inc.; SportsLight: Brian Drake, Long Photography; Wide World Photos.

Printed in the United States of America.

Library of Congress Cataloging-in-Publication Data

Rambeck, Richard.

Minnesota Timberwolves / Richard Rambeck.

Summary: A history of the Minnesota Timberwolves, the second NBA team to be based in Minnesota's Twin Cities.

ISBN 0-88682-524-5

1. Minnesota Timberwolves (Basketball team)—History—Juvenile literature. [1. Minnesota Timberwolves (Basketball team)—History. 02. Basketball—History.] I. Title.

GV885.52.M565R36 1992 92-4114
796.323'64'09776579—dc20 CIP

MINNESOTA: HOME OF THE TIMBERWOLVES

Minnesota's Twin Cities—Minneapolis and St. Paul—are the two largest urban areas in the state with the nicknames "North Star State" and the "Gopher State." In fact, the Twin Cities metropolitan area accounts for more than half of the 4.3 million people who live in Minnesota. The Twin Cities are located on the eastern edge of the state, along the Mississippi River and near the Minnesota-Wisconsin border. The Mississippi actually divides the two cities: Minneapolis is on the west side of the river, and St. Paul is on the east.

Because of their proximity to the United States' longest river, the Twin Cities are centers of maritime activity. Several major barge lines operate out of Minneapolis and St. Paul,

The home of the Timberwolves.

carrying goods down the mighty Mississippi to other freshwater ports. In addition, St. Paul is the capital of Minnesota, so it is home to the governor and the state legislature.

Former Lakers star George Mikan headed a panel appointed in 1984 to help bring basketball back to Minnesota.

The Twin Cities area has also been a center of professional team sports. Based there are the Minnesota Vikings of the National Football League, the Minnesota Twins of baseball's American League, and the Minnesota North Stars of the National Hockey League. But Minnesota's first professional sports team didn't play football, baseball, or hockey. The Minneapolis Lakers played basketball and were among the charter members of the National Basketball Association in the late 1940s.

In the early years of the NBA, the Minneapolis Lakers were the dominant club in the league. Led by 6-foot-10 center George Mikan, Minneapolis won an amazing five league titles between 1949 and 1954, failing only to claim the 1950-51 championship. But Mikan retired after the 1953-54 season, and the Lakers were never the same—at least not in Minnesota. Fewer and fewer people attended Laker games. By the end of the 1959-60 season, the owners of the team decided to move the club to Los Angeles.

After the Lakers moved west, fans in Minnesota found teams in other sports to cheer for. By the mid-1980s, however, business leaders in the Twin Cities area believed it was time to bring an NBA club back to Minnesota. When the league announced plans to add two to four new teams, two Twin Cities businessmen vowed to win one of those expansion franchises for their state.

Tod Murphy, a Timberwolves original.

WOLVES
4
LAKERS

BRINGING BASKETBALL BACK TO MINNESOTA

In early 1987, work began on a new arena, the Target Center, located in downtown Minneapolis.

Landing an NBA team for the Twin Cities was a longtime dream for Harvey Ratner and Marv Wolfenson, avid sports fans who had spent their lives in the area. They had been friends since childhood and business partners since 1952. Both of them remembered the glory days of George Mikan and the Minneapolis Lakers. Ratner and Wolfenson had built a successful business empire around a chain of health clubs in the Twin Cities. Now they wanted to build an NBA team.

The two partners began raising money and making plans for the new franchise. Luckily, they didn't have to look far to find a sports expert to run the organization. Bob Stein, who was married to Wolfenson's daughter, had been an All-American football player at the University of Minnesota and later played for the Kansas City Chiefs in the National Football League. Stein had become a successful businessman after his football career and was a natural to run a pro sports franchise. He was appointed president of the team.

One of Stein's first duties was finding a nickname for the franchise. He held a name-the-team contest in December 1986 and received more than 6,000 entries. The two most popular choices were Timberwolves and Polars, both of which suggested Minnesota's northern location and cold winter weather. After consulting with city officials from all over the state, Stein decided on Timberwolves, animals that are fairly common in the northern part of the country.

With the team nickname decided, Stein set about making sure that the NBA granted Minnesota a team. But there was really never any doubt. Most of the NBA owners and officials believed it was only fair to return a franchise to the area that had produced the league's first great team. On April 3, 1987, NBA commissioner David Stern announced that the Minnesota Timberwolves would begin playing in the 1989-90 season. Minnesota would enter the league the same year as the Orlando Magic.

During Bill Musselman's four seasons in the CBA, he was twice chosen Coach of the Year.

MUSSELMAN PROVIDES COACHING STRENGTH

Minnesota had its NBA franchise, but club leaders still had their work cut out for them. They had only a year and a half to put the pieces together for the Timberwolves' initial season in the league. Their first task was to find a head coach. Club president Bob Stein had his eye on a man who had won four professional basketball championships with four different teams in four years. The man's name was Bill Musselman, and he already had strong ties to the Twin Cities area. In the early 1970s, Musselman had been a successful coach at the University of Minnesota.

Basketball fans knew Musselman even better as a professional coach than as a college mentor. He had an impressive record as a head coach in the Continental Basketball Association, a minor pro league. The CBA was made up of young players and NBA castoffs who dreamed of making the big time. The CBA was a troubled league, however. Financial difficulties often forced CBA teams to move from city to city; sometimes, the teams just went out of business.

This explains how Musselman could have coached four different teams to CBA championships in four straight years. He won league titles while coaching Sarasota (Florida), Tampa Bay (Florida), Rapid City (South Dakota), and Albany (New York). Musselman's 1987-88 Albany team posted an amazing 48-6 record, the best single-season

Center Felton Spencer.

Australian native Luc Longley.

Sam Mitchell sank the Timberwolves' first basket in the team's opening game on November 3, 1989.

winning percentage ever recorded by a pro basketball club in the United States.

What was Musselman's secret to success? He preached hard work and hustle on defense, and discipline and patience on offense. Musselman's teams rarely ran fast breaks. Their games were low-scoring, but his teams usually wound up with the highest point total in the end. Stein believed this system would be good for an expansion team that would not be able to gather much talent in its first few years.

Musselman was named head coach of the Timberwolves during a press conference on August 23, 1988. He walked up to the microphone and left no doubt about the kind of team that he expected the Timberwolves to be: a hard-nosed, Bill Musselman-type defensive ball club.

"What will the team be like?" Musselman asked. "Visualize a cold, dark night in the state of Minnesota. A pack of timberwolves is stalking and waiting for its prey. And the prey—and opposition—is fearful of what might happen. World War III will take place. In lighter terms, the prey is in for a tough night and the battle of its life."

Former University of Minnesota star Randy Breuer returned home in January 1990 as part of the club's first trade.

Musselman then explained the type of player he wanted for his team. "You want people that know how to play the game," he said. "Game intelligence is very important. A lot of people play the game, but very few know how to play it. I think intelligence and character are important. You also have to get players that other people like to play with. We want good people with character and work habits who'll be playing in the league for eight to ten years, providing they don't get hurt."

Musselman and Stein would have to select their ideal players from two main sources: the college draft and the league expansion draft. In the expansion draft, each NBA team would be allowed to "protect" eight of the 12 players on its roster. One of the remaining four from each team could be drafted by Minnesota or Orlando, the other expansion team that would start play in the 1989-90 season.

LANDING A HIDDEN GEM: TYRONE CORBIN

The Timberwolves would be able to acquire about a dozen players in the expansion draft, but Musselman wasn't expecting to find many potential stars. He figured the team would get one, two, or maybe three young veterans who could fit into his system. Luckily, the Timberwolves did find one really solid player: 6-foot-6 forward Tyrone Corbin, who had been a part-time starter for the powerful Phoenix Suns during the 1988-89 season. The Suns had liked Corbin's hustle and rebounding ability; they also liked the fact that he was unselfish. Phoenix didn't ask Corbin to score a lot, just to rebound and play tough defense.

Tyrone Corbin's nine steals during a 1990 game against Dallas is still a club record.

Musselman was surprised when the Suns didn't protect Corbin in the expansion draft. Corbin, Musselman believed, was just the type of player to fit into Minnesota's defense-oriented system. "We got a guy who was a starting forward on a team that won 55 games," Musselman said gleefully. "He's a tremendous role player. We're looking for over-achievers. To be the leading offensive rebounder at 6-foot-6 on a great team, that tells you something." Apparently, Musselman wasn't the only NBA coach who coveted Corbin. "We had 11 teams call up and ask about him," Musselman said, explaining that those clubs wanted to trade for Corbin. But Minnesota wasn't about to part with its highly rated pick.

GETTING TO THE POINT WITH POOH

With Corbin on board, Musselman's next task was finding talent in the NBA college draft. Selecting in the middle of the first round, the Timberwolves surprised many experts by taking UCLA point guard Jerome "Pooh" Richardson. Some of those experts believed that Richardson wasn't even first-round material. They pointed to his erratic shooting and questionable defense. One expert said that if the Timberwolves really wanted Richardson, they could have waited and picked him in the second round of the draft—because he still would have been available.

The hustling Tyrone Corbin.

WOLVES
23
31
CURRY
30

Pooh Richardson was elected to the NBA's 1989-90 All-Rookie first team.

Musselman, however, didn't believe what he heard about Richardson. The Minnesota coach was impressed by the way the guard handled himself on the court. "He likes to lead," Musselman explained. "He makes decisions on the court as well as anybody. He's an extremely confident kid. He has an attitude about him that just reeks of confidence. And he knows the game. You sit down and talk to him, and he talks the game much beyond his age."

Richardson was happy to be going to Minnesota because he knew he wouldn't be a bench sitter. "It's a great opportunity," he explained. "You get to learn a lot by playing a lot. I feel great about going there." Richardson also said he was looking forward to taking control of the Timberwolves' offense. "I want to be depended on," he said. "I like the challenge."

Pooh Richardson, former Minnesota point guard.

Center Felton Spencer wins the tip.

24
WOLVES
50
FOOT LOCKER

In 1989-90, Sam Mitchell finished fifth among all NBA rookies in scoring and fourth in rebounding.

MITCHELL FINALLY FINDS A HOME IN THE NBA

Meanwhile, coach Musselman had his own challenge. He was trying to find other players who could help the team. He believed he could find hidden talent among players who had been in the CBA. And, thanks to his many years as a coach in the CBA, nobody knew the league as well as Musselman did.

As it turned out, most of Minnesota's players during the team's first season were former CBA stars. One of those players was forward Sam Mitchell, who had tried for years to make an NBA team. When he graduated from tiny Mercer College in Macon, Georgia, in 1985, Mitchell joined the Army. But his love of basketball soon took over. He was granted a discharge from the Army and wound up playing for clubs in the CBA and the U.S. Basketball League, a summer league for players hoping to impress NBA scouts.

Musselman had coached Mitchell while both were with the Tampa Bay Thrillers for the 1986-87 season. After that, Musselman lost contact with Mitchell, who left the United States to play in France for a year. In the summer of 1989, the Minnesota coach heard that Mitchell would be attending a rookie tryout camp. Musselman sent Billy McKinney, the Timberwolves' director of player personnel, to see if Mitchell was in shape to play in the NBA. As soon as McKinney saw Mitchell, he knew the 6-foot-7 forward was NBA material.

Tony Campbell ranked 11th in the league in 1989-90 in points scored (1,903).

McKinney pulled Mitchell out of a pregame layup drill and asked him if he would be willing to sign with the Timberwolves. Mitchell didn't waste any time: He placed the contract on McKinney's back and signed it right then. The contract didn't promise Mitchell several million dollars, but it did offer him a chance to finally play in the NBA. "It isn't about money," Mitchell explained. "It's about showing people that I should have been here four years ago."

Mitchell had worked hard, against long odds, to get a chance in the NBA. When he joined the Timberwolves, he was surrounded by players who had no idea what it was like to be in the minor leagues of pro basketball. "I hear rookies say, 'I'd never play in the CBA,'" Mitchell recalled. "Good! Don't if you don't have to. But then you can't know what it's like to work in a place where everybody's goal is to get out." After four years of trying, Mitchell had finally escaped.

The high-scoring Tony Campbell.

TONY CAMPBELL GETS HIS CHANCE

Two months after Mitchell signed with Minnesota, the Timberwolves offered a new home to another player who was trying to establish an NBA career, shooting guard Tony Campbell. Unlike Mitchell, Campbell had prior NBA experience. He had been the 1984 first-round draft choice of the Detroit Pistons. Campbell couldn't crack the lineup in Detroit, however, so he moved on to the Los Angeles Lakers, where he backed up James Worthy and Byron Scott for several years. Los Angeles let him go after the 1988-89 season.

Tod Murphy grabbed a club-record 20 rebounds during a January 1990 game against the Los Angeles Clippers.

After being cut by the Lakers, Campbell wondered if he would ever be an NBA star. He knew he could score and score a lot, but nobody had ever given him much of a chance. He hoped that would change in Minnesota. During the Timberwolves' first season, Musselman put Campbell in the starting lineup and left him there. Campbell responded by averaging 23.2 points a game, the 14th-highest average in the league. He scored at least 10 points in every game of the season, and topped the Timberwolves in scoring in 55 of 82 contests.

Led by Campbell's scoring and the hustle of Mitchell and Corbin, the Timberwolves became a very popular ticket in the Twin Cities. Minnesota played the 1989-90 season in the Metrodome, a giant indoor stadium designed for football and baseball. Fans flocked to the Metrodome in record numbers. On November 10, 1989, a record crowd of more than 29,000 was on hand to see the "T-wolves" make history. That night, Campbell scored 38 points and Corbin added 36 as Minnesota shocked powerful Philadelphia, beating the 76ers 125-118 in overtime. It was the Timberwolves' first NBA victory.

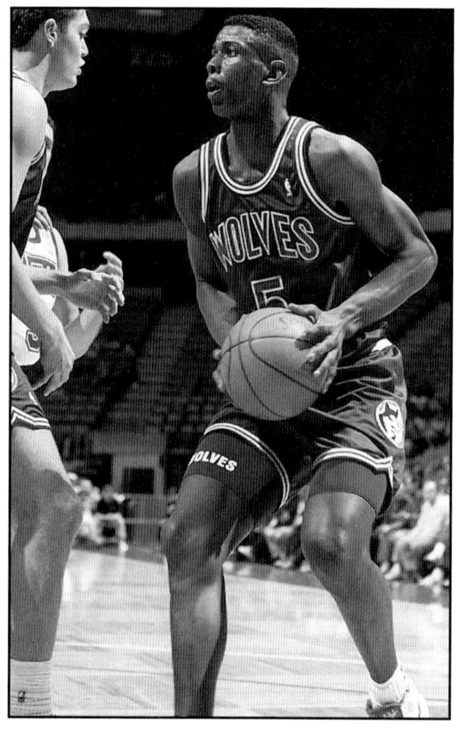

 Left to right: Doug West, Randy Breuer, Gerald Glass, Scott Brooks.

But the highlight of the Timberwolves' first season came in February. Minnesota posted a 6-7 record during the month, including a 116-105 victory over the Boston Celtics and Larry Bird. More than 35,000 people watched that game in the Metrodome. In March, more than 43,000 fans came to see the Timberwolves nearly upset the Lakers, who were led by Magic Johnson. Minnesota lost 101-98 in front of the largest crowd in the NBA so far that season. And the Twin Cities fans were just warming up.

Tony Campbell scored 44 points, still a team record, in the T-Wolves' victory over Boston in February 1990.

In April, 49,551 people attended a game between Minnesota and the Denver Nuggets. It was the third-largest single-game attendance total in league history. Later that month, 45,458 Timberwolves fans watched their team defeat the Orlando Magic, a fellow expansion franchise, by a score of 117-102. It was Minnesota's 22nd victory of the season, the most among the four new teams in the NBA.

The Timberwolves finished their initial season in the NBA with a 22-60 record, an excellent mark for a first-year team. But the biggest news wasn't Minnesota's success on the court; rather, it was the team's success at the ticket booth. The Timberwolves set an NBA single-season record by drawing 1,072,572 fans, an average of more than 26,000 a game.

Minnesota wouldn't be able to match that mark in the team's second year, however. That was because the Timberwolves were moving into the newly built Target Center, which had a seating capacity of 18,000, far less than the Metrodome. The arena might have been smaller than the Metrodome, but it was a beautiful new home that was designed especially for basketball.

Pooh Richardson (pages 26-27).

WOLVES
24

FELTON SPENCER FINDS HIS CONFIDENCE

Felton Spencer's 121 blocks in 1990-91 placed him among the league leaders.

In addition to a new home, the Timberwolves also had a new center for the 1990-91 season. Minnesota used its first-round pick in the 1990 college draft to take 7-foot Felton Spencer of the University of Louisville. Spencer was a late bloomer who didn't play much basketball while growing up. At Louisville, he made major improvements in his game. "It's as though he's found himself," said Billy McKinney, Minnesota's director of player personnel. "He has a self-confidence that he didn't have even in his early years in college."

Spencer was much improved, but McKinney knew he probably wasn't a potential superstar. "I have a feeling Spencer is going to be a very good center for a long time," McKinney predicted. "But if you expect greatness from him, then you're likely to be disappointed." Spencer wasn't great during his rookie year, but he was solid. He played in all 82 games for Minnesota and was a starter in 60. The center averaged 7.1 points and led the team in rebounds by grabbing almost eight a game. Spencer's efforts landed him a spot on the NBA All-Rookie second team.

Despite Spencer's solid play, the Timberwolves struggled during the early part of the 1990-91 season. Coach Bill Musselman's defense-minded strategy made it tough for the opponents to score, but Minnesota was having an even harder time putting the ball in the basket. During one 12-game stretch, the Timberwolves scored only 86.6 points a contest, about 20 below the league average. But things changed on December 30, 1990. In the locker room before a game with Seattle, Musselman walked up to point guard Pooh Richardson and said, "Let's run."

Richardson was delighted. The Timberwolves would get to pick up the pace, which was exactly what the second-year guard wanted. That night Minnesota demolished Seattle 126-106. The new-look Timberwolves improved rapidly behind Richardson, who wound up the season averaging 17.1 points and almost nine assists a game. Tony Campbell topped the team in scoring once again with a 21.8 average. Tyrone Corbin chipped in 18 points a game and was Minnesota's second-leading rebounder.

Pooh Richardson started every game during the T-Wolves' first three seasons.

A NEW LEADER AND A NEW STYLE FOR THE FUTURE

The Timberwolves finished the 1990-91 season with a 29-53 record, an improvement of seven victories over their first-year mark. Despite the better record, the Timberwolves decided to fire coach Bill Musselman. The coach and team management differed on how to develop the club. Musselman wanted to win right away; other team officials wanted him to use younger players more often and build for the future. Musselman was replaced by Jimmy Rodgers, former head coach of the Boston Celtics.

"I'm not here to do anything but win," Rodgers said. "But I do understand that to move along, you have to take care of the franchise's building blocks, your young players. . . . And, oh yes, we will run with the basketball." That was welcome news to Timberwolves players such as Pooh Richardson and Tony Campbell, who had resented Musselman's slow-down approach to offense.

With Rodgers at the helm and with the addition of power forward Thurl Bailey and rookie center Luc Longley, the Timberwolves believe they can be a playoff contender in the near future. The 6-foot-11 Bailey, obtained in a trade

Rising talent Doug West.

Minnesota's hope for the future, Christian Laettner.

Thurl Bailey averaged over 11 points in 1991-92 and was high in the voting for the NBA's Sixth Man award.

with the Utah Jazz for Tyrone Corbin, is both an inside and outside threat. The T-Wolves are counting on him to provide more rebounding and offensive firepower than Corbin did. Longley, a 7-foot-2 Australian, is a talented but not yet dominant player. He needs to work on his inside game, his shot-blocking, and his defense. But Rodgers, who has had a lot of experience helping NBA centers improve, is willing to give Longley time to work on his game. As an assistant coach with Boston, Rodgers oversaw the development of another raw talent, Robert Parish, who is now one of the best centers in the NBA.

If Longley and Minnesota's other fine young players do live up to their potential, the Timberwolves could match the success of that other Minnesota NBA basketball team of old, the Minneapolis Lakers. The Lakers also built their squad around a giant center—George Mikan—and rode with him to the top of the NBA. The Timberwolves are counting on Luc Longley to help them rewrite that success story in the Twin Cities.